ABOUT THE BANK STREET READY-TO-READ SERIES

Seventy years of educational research and innovative teaching have given the Bank Street College of Education the reputation as America's most trusted name in early childhood education.

Because no two children are exactly alike in their development, we have designed the *Bank Street Ready-to-Read* series in three levels to accommodate the individual stages of reading readiness of children ages four through eight.

- ● *Level 1:* GETTING READY TO READ—read-alouds for children who are taking their first steps toward reading.
- ● *Level 2:* READING TOGETHER—for children who are just beginning to read by themselves but may need a little help.
- ○ *Level 3:* I CAN READ IT MYSELF—for children who can read independently.

Our three levels make it easy to select the books most appropriate for a child's development and enable him or her to grow with the series step by step. The *Bank Street Ready-to-Read* books also overlap and reinforce each other, further encouraging the reading process.

We feel that making reading fun and enjoyable is the single most important thing that you can do to help children become good readers. And we hope you'll be a part of Bank Street's long tradition of learning through sharing.

The Bank Street College of Education

For David Glen Bunn III
—W.H.H.

*For all
the Mr. (and Ms.) Baseballs
everywhere*
—P.M.

MR. BASEBALL
A Bantam Little Rooster Book/November 1991

*Little Rooster is a trademark of Bantam Books,
a division of Bantam Doubleday Dell Publishing Group, Inc.*

*Series graphic design by Alex Jay/Studio J
Editor: Gillian Bucky*

*Special thanks to James A. Levine, Betsy Gould,
Sally Doherty, and Whit Stillman.*

Library of Congress Cataloging-in-Publication Data
Hooks, William H.
Mr. Baseball / by William H. Hooks ;
illustrated by Paul Meisel.
p. cm. — (Bank Street ready-to-read)
''A Byron Preiss book.''
Summary: A Little Leaguer suffers the
enthusiastic activities of his
baseball-loving five-year-old brother.
ISBN 0-553-07315-X. — ISBN 0-553-35303-9 (pbk.)
[1. Baseball—Fiction. 2. Brothers—Fiction.]
I. Meisel, Paul, ill. II. Title.
III. Title: Mister Baseball. IV. Series.
PZ7.H7664Mp 1991
[E]—dc20

90-43303 CIP AC

Published simultaneously in the United States and Canada

*Bantam Books are published by Bantam Books, a division of Bantam Doubleday
Dell Publishing Group, Inc. Its trademark, consisting of the words ''Bantam Books''
and the portrayal of a rooster, is Registered in U.S. Patent and Trademark Office
and in other countries. Marca Registrada. Bantam Books, 666 Fifth Avenue, New
York, New York 10103.*

PRINTED IN THE UNITED STATES OF AMERICA

0 9 8 7 6 5 4 3 2 1

Bank Street Ready-to-Read™

Mr. Baseball

by William H. Hooks
Illustrated by Paul Meisel

A Byron Preiss Book

A BANTAM LITTLE ROOSTER BOOK
NEW YORK · TORONTO · LONDON · SYDNEY · AUCKLAND

4

Mr. Baseball

My brother Eli is five years old,
and he gets stuck on things.
He used to be stuck on me.
That kid stuck to me like
a piece of chewing gum.
I even named him Mr. Bubble Gum.

Then Eli got stuck on monsters.
Our room looked like a monster zoo.
I changed his name to Mr. Monster.

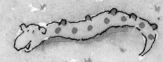

Now he's stuck on baseball.

Does he know any
of the rules?
Can he pitch or catch?

Is he old enough for Little League?
No!
But I've given him a new name anyway—
Mr. Baseball.

Chickens and Wildcats

Last night, Eli said to me,
"I'm joining Little League."
"Ha." I laughed.
"You must mean the Pee Wees."
"No," said Eli, "Little League."
"They don't take five year olds," I said.
"I'm joining anyway," said Eli.
I saw that stubborn look on his face,
so I didn't argue.

On Saturday I called my friend Roberta.
"What's up?" asked Roberta.
"Brother trouble," I said.
"Is Eli into monsters again?" she asked.
"No," I said, "now it's baseball."
"Great!" said Roberta.
"He can watch the Roosters with us."

"No," I groaned.
"Eli is not into watching.
He's into joining!"
"Bring Eli over here," said Roberta.
"I've got a cure for him
and a surprise for you."

On the way over I told Eli,
"We're going to watch the Roosters
on TV."
"It's no good on TV," mumbled Eli.

12

Roberta met us outside her house.
"Surprise!" she shouted.
"We've got tickets to the Roosters.
Mom's taking all of us!"
"The real live Roosters?" asked Eli.
"You bet!" said Roberta.

Roberta's mom pulled up to the curb.
"Hop in, kids, and buckle up!" she said.
Eli was so excited,
he needed a seat belt
to hold him down.

At the ballpark I said to Roberta,
"This is going to make things worse
with Eli."
"Don't worry," said Roberta.
"But we'll never keep him away
from Little League now," I said.
"Don't worry," Roberta said again.
"This is going to be a long game.
Little kids like Eli get tired and bored.
He'll be asleep halfway
through the game."

Well, I did worry.
Roberta and I had just made
Little League.
The last thing I needed was
a little brother underfoot.

16

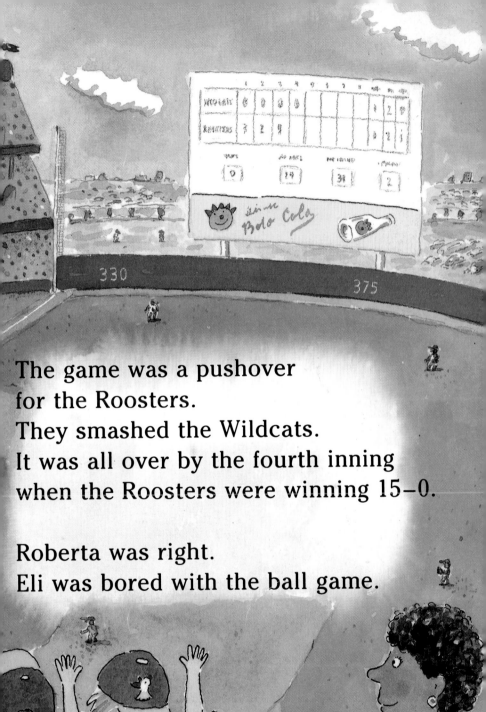

The game was a pushover
for the Roosters.
They smashed the Wildcats.
It was all over by the fourth inning
when the Roosters were winning 15–0.

Roberta was right.
Eli was bored with the ball game.

17

But she hadn't counted on the mascots.
The Roosters had a guy dressed
like a chicken.

The Wildcats had someone
dressed up like an alley cat.

18

Eli kept jabbing me.
"Look at that chicken!" he cried.
"That's the mascot for the Roosters,"
I explained.
The chicken turned a cartwheel.
"Hooray!" yelled Eli.
"Shut up!" I said.

Everyone else was holding their breath
watching a Rooster player slide
into home plate.
The crowd went wild.
The chicken turned another cartwheel.
"Go, chicken, go!" yelled Eli.

It was the same with the Wildcat mascot.
The cat did back flips.
Eli cheered the cat
while the Wildcat fans moaned
as their batter struck out.

Roberta was right again.
After a hot dog and a soda,
Eli went to sleep.
He had a nice, long nap
while we watched a boring game.

Roberta's mom drove us home.
I thought Roberta's cure had worked.
But as we got out of the car Eli said,
"I'm going to be the mascot
of the Little League team."
I looked at Roberta.
"Some cure you came up with," I said.

Water Boy

I tried to sneak out of the house,
but it's hard when you are carrying
a bat, a glove, two balls,
and wearing a Little League uniform.
It's even harder if your little brother
is watching every move you make.
"Okay," I said to Eli.
"You win, Mr. Baseball. Come on."

Roberta was warming up
when we got to the playing field.
She pitched a fast ball
to Coach Hardee.
"Way to go, Roberta!" yelled Eli.

27

Eli ran over to Coach Hardee and said,
"Hi, Coach. Give me five!"
Coach Hardee looked down at Eli
and frowned.
Then he broke into a big smile.
He slapped Eli's hand and said,
"Gotcha! All five!
What's your name, shortstop?" he asked.
Eli flashed a big smile and said,
"My name is Eli.
But you can call me Mr. Baseball."
Coach Hardee roared with laughter.

"I'm joining Little League," said Eli.
"Is that so?" asked Coach Hardee.
"Yep," said Eli.
"Tell you what," said Coach Hardee.
"Why don't you help me on the sidelines.
Get the feel of the game."
I couldn't believe my ears.
Coach Hardee is a real tough guy,
but he was a pushover for Eli.
"See that water bucket over there,"
said the coach.
"You're in charge, Eli.
You're the water boy for the day."

It turned out to be the hottest day ever.
Eli was one busy water boy,
and the coach was his best customer.

Coach Hardee gets very excited,
especially when he's trying
to whip us into shape.
He was running up and down,
waving his arms and shouting.
Eli was right behind him.
Everything the coach said, Eli repeated.

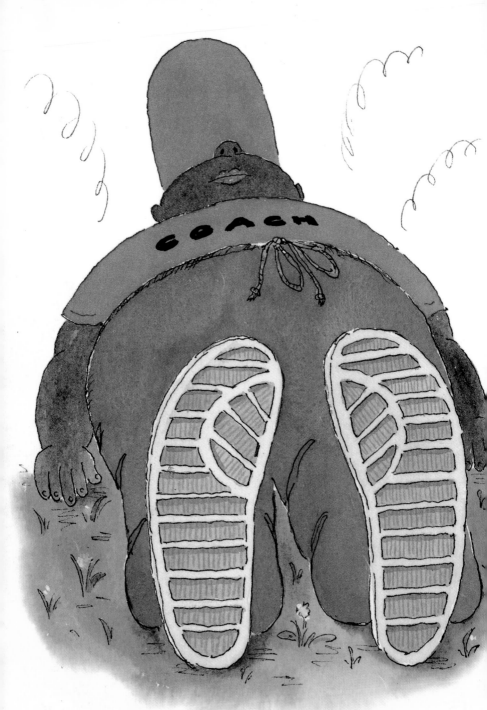

Suddenly, Coach Hardee toppled over.
The game stopped.

34

For a moment nobody moved.
Then we all crowded around the coach.
Everyone was talking at once.
"What happened?"
"Did he faint?"
"Do we need a doctor?"

"Gangway! Gangway!" someone yelled.
The circle around the coach opened up.
In dashed Eli
with his water bucket.
Splash!

He dumped the water
on the coach's head.
The coach sat up.
He shook the water from his face.
He looked at Eli and said,
"Thanks, pal,
I needed that!"

The Mascot

Eli went to Little League practice
for two weeks.
Then he stopped.
"Where's our water boy?"
asked the coach.
"I guess he got bored," I said.
Coach Hardee looked sad.

"I told you he would get bored,"
said Roberta.
"Eli is up to something," I said.

40

"Good," said Roberta.
"Bad," I answered.
"He still wants to join Little League."

Finally we were ready for our first game.
All of our moms and dads
and friends came to the game.
"Is Eli coming?" asked Roberta.
"Mom's bringing him," I answered.

We ran out onto the field.
All of our friends yelled.
Then the crowd yelled louder.
"What are they yelling for?"
I asked Roberta.

"That!" said Roberta.

She pointed at a huge baseball.
It had two feet at the bottom,
an arm at each side,
and one head sticking out of the top!

"Oh, no!" I cried.
"Mr. Baseball strikes again!"

Eli ran down the field.
He turned a cartwheel—sort of.
But the crowd roared.
Coach Hardee roared louder
than anyone.
"We've got ourselves a mascot,"
he yelled.

We won our first game,
thanks to Roberta's great pitching.

Eli was made the team mascot,
thanks to Mom's help with his costume.

Our mascot got a name: Mr. Baseball—
thanks to me.